WELCOME HOME, BIG BIRD

By EMILY PERL KINGSLEY ◆ *Illustrated by* TOM COOKE

Featuring Jim Henson's
Sesame Street Muppets

Inspired by SESAME STREET PRESENTS: FOLLOW THAT BIRD,
screenplay by Tony Geiss and Judy Freudberg

A SESAME STREET / GOLDEN PRESS BOOK
Published by Western Publishing Company, Inc.
in conjunction with Children's Television Workshop

"Gee, Ernie," said Bert, "it sure is different on Sesame Street when Big Bird isn't around!"

"Right, Bert!" said Ernie. "How long has he been gone, anyway?"

David looked at the calendar. "He's been gone only two weeks," he said.

"But when you miss somebody," said Betty Lou, "it always seems longer."

The door to Hooper's Store opened and Grover came running in. "Look, everybody!" he shouted. "Here is a postcard from Big Bird!"

Grover read the postcard. " 'Dear Ernie, Bert, Telly, Oscar, Grover, Cookie Monster, Mr. Snuffle-upagus, Prairie Dawn, Herry Monster, Betty Lou, Forgetful Jones, Sherlock Hemlock, Biff, Barkley, Sully, Grundgetta, Slimey, Count, and all the Honkers...' "

Grover stopped.

"Yes, yes," Bert said impatiently. "Dear everybody. Okay, but what does he say?"

"I am afraid that is all he had room for on the postcard," Grover said sadly. "That is it."

"Gee," said Ernie, "that was a very nice postcard, but we still don't know when Big Bird is coming home!"

Just then Prairie Dawn ran into the store. "Hey, everybody," she cried. "Here's a postcard from Big Bird!"

"My, my," said the Count. "Two postcards in one day!"

" 'Dear all those people on my first postcard,' " Prairie Dawn read out loud. " 'How are you? I am fine. I've had a good time, but now I'm coming home. I miss you. I'll be home Wednesday afternoon. Love, Big Bird. P.S. Do you miss me?' "

"What a silly question," said Betty Lou. "Of course we miss him! I've missed sitting curled up in his nest, listening to him read his poems."

"I've missed him coming in for his daily birdseed sandwich with a birdseed soda on the side," said David. "I haven't sold a single birdseed sandwich in two weeks!"

"I've missed going down to
the park with him to talk to the
pigeons," said Bert. "In fact,
I'm sure even the *pigeons* missed
him!"

"And I've missed playing
hide-and-seek with him," said
Prairie Dawn.

Everybody thought about the special things they had missed while Big Bird was away.

Suddenly Forgetful Jones jumped up. "I have an idea!" he shouted. "How about having a Welcome Home party for... uh...who's coming home?"

"Big Bird!" said Herry.

"That is a terrific idea, Forgetful," said Grover. "A party for Big Bird!"

"Then we can all show him how much we missed him while he was away," said Bert.

"We need lots of good stuff to eat!" said Cookie Monster.

"And decorations!" said Betty Lou.

Meanwhile, Big Bird was on his way home on a big bus. "Gee, Radar," he said to his teddy bear, "I sure can't wait to get home. I missed everybody so much that I'm coming home six hours early."

The bus pulled up at the Sesame Street bus stop. Big Bird got off the bus with his suitcase and Radar.

"That's funny," he said. "I was sure everybody would be waiting here to meet me." He looked down Sesame Street.

Big Bird's friends were working so hard that they didn't see him.

"Gosh, Radar," said Big Bird. "No wonder nobody came to meet me. Everyone is busy getting ready for some big party. They're all blowing up balloons and hanging paper streamers and everything. I wonder who the party is for."

Big Bird peeked through the window of Hooper's Store. "Look at all the food they're making!" he said. "Sandwiches and salad and...wow, look at that fancy cake!"

Big Bird took a closer look. He blinked his eyes. "That's a *birdseed* layer cake!" he cried. "And those are *birdseed*-and-watercress sandwiches. Those are my favorite bird foods! This party must be for some very important bird. I wonder who it could be."

Big Bird looked around the corner and saw Telly, Herry, and the kids painting a sign.

"I guess the minute I was gone everyone forgot all about me. I guess they found themselves a whole new bird. And now they're having a big party to welcome this new bird to Sesame Street!"

Big Bird was feeling more and more sad.

"Look at that sign they're painting," he said miserably. "It says, 'WELCOME H.' That new bird's name must be Harvey or Henrietta or something that starts with the letter H."

Big Bird peeked over the fence at his own nest. Mr. Snuffle-upagus was busy decorating the nest with colorful streamers and balloons.

"Oh, no!" said Big Bird. "Even my best friend Mr. Snuffle-upagus has forgotten all about me. He's getting my nest ready for that new bird on Sesame Street."

Big Bird's beak trembled and his eyes filled with tears. He walked slowly back to the bus stop.

Just as Big Bird was about to get on the bus and ride away
from Sesame Street forever, Prairie Dawn looked up and saw
him.

"Hey, Big Bird!" she cried. "Look everybody, there's Big
Bird! He's about to get on that bus!"

Prairie Dawn ran down Sesame Street toward the bus stop.
"Big Bird, wait!" she called.

"Big Bird," said Bert, "what are you doing here? Your postcard said you weren't coming home until this afternoon!"

"What do you care?" Big Bird said, with a tear sliding down his beak. "You didn't miss me at all! You're too busy making birdseed sandwiches and birdseed cake and a big sign saying WELCOME H for some new bird whose name starts with H who is coming to Sesame Street to take my place!"

"What?" said Betty Lou. "Oh. That sign is finished now. Would you like to see what it says?"

" 'WELCOME HOME, BIG BIRD!' Ohhhhh. That 'H' was the first letter in the word HOME!" Then Big Bird looked at the beautiful decorations. "You mean the party was for me?"

"Who else, you big turkey," said Oscar. "Who else likes birdseed layer cake?"

"And the birdseed sandwiches are for me, too?" asked Big Bird. "And the balloons? And the streamers?"

"Yes, Big Bird," said Prairie Dawn.

"One hundred twenty-four balloons!" shouted the Count. "Eighty-seven streamers! Only one cake, but forty-three sandwiches!"

"If you did all this for me, does it mean that you missed me?" Big Bird asked.

"We all missed you very much," answered David.

"Well, what are we waiting for?" shouted Big Bird. "Let's have a party!"

"We thought you'd never ask," said Cookie Monster.

And so there was a happy Welcome Home party
for Big Bird on Sesame Street.

Big Bird slept in his own nest that night.
It was good to be home.

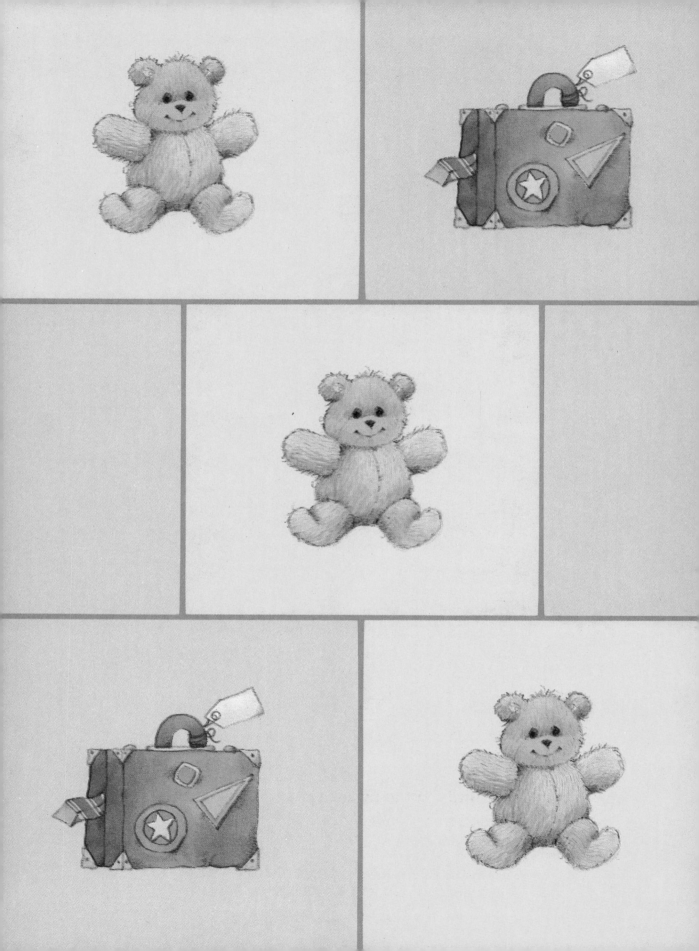